I0534340

Tomoiya's Story:

Collecting Tears

By

C. A. King

Cover Design: Just Write Creations

Editor: J.D. Cunegan

*This book is dedicated to readers everywhere. Without you,
my novels would be nothing more than words on a blank page.*

-and-

To the people who have never given up on me, even in the rough times!

Look for other books by C.A. King, including:

The Portal Prophecies:
Book I - A Keeper's Destiny
Book II - A Halloween's Curse
Book III - Frost Bitten
Book IV - Sleeping Sands
Book V - Deadly Perceptions
Book VI - Finding Balance

Tomoiya's Story:

Book I: Escape to Darkness
Book II: Collecting Tears

Surviving the Sins:

Book I: Answering the Call
Book II: Pride
Book III: Lust

When Leaves Fall: A Different Point of View Story

Peach Coloured Daisies: A Cursed by the Gods Story

Flower Shields: A Four Horsemen Novel

Drawing Strength From Words: A Four Horsemen Novel

Miracles Not Included

Twisted Tales of A Dead End Street
Shot Through The Heart: A Faerie Tale

Cover Design: **Just Write Creations**

Second Printing: August 2017
Third Printing: July 2018

ISBN 978-1-988301-13-6

Kings Toe Publishing
kingstoepublishing@gmail.com
Burlington, Ontario. Canada

Chapter One

Her hands smoothed over the red gown that covered her school uniform. For a split second she thought about the cap. As pretty as it was with its golden tassel hanging down, she knew her hair underneath was suffering. Inhaling deeply, she cleared her mind.

Meditation equals concentration.

"You'll be brilliant!" Moira exclaimed.

She smiled - not a happy smile, but rather an obligatory one. Reassurances weren't something she needed. There had been hundreds of speeches over the short span of her lifetime - each one articulated perfectly. This would be a walk in the park in comparison.

"Tomoiya and Moira," the headmaster called, followed by a loud applause. That was their cue.

There was a time, not long ago, when the lectern had concealed her body from the audience. That wasn't the case anymore. In fact, standing on a podium suited her frame perfectly. She chalked it up to experience.

Those around her, however, tended to disagree. There was a gracefulness in everything she did that screamed royalty.

It was that quality that brought the entire student body to this school to learn. After four years, Tomoiya still wasn't sure it was something that could be taught.

Rule number two - a princess never needed to announce her title. Royalty was recognized, not demanded.

"Good afternoon," Tomoiya said, looking out into a sea of her peers. Hundreds of pairs of eyes returned her gaze, without a blink in sight. Each set was poised on the cusp of anticipation - patiently awaiting every word that escaped her pink lips. Those in front of her were the future - each one either part of a royal line or destined to be an important leader. Moira echoed her greeting.

"Valedictorian," Tomoiya began, "the word itself inspires. There is no greater honour after four long years, than to stand before you: my teachers; mentors; peers; friends; and family. This moment is only made better by having my best friend, Moira, at my side to join in the honour."

"In a way we've been given a nod and in return, we'd like to give one to the future," Moira continued. "We have spent our high school lives learning. Not just about math and language, but about each other as well. The connections we have made here will last a lifetime."

"In essence, each of us has drawn an outline - a plan to follow throughout our lives. In the years to come, we will be the rulers of the planets, kingdoms, realms and companies that make up the known Universe. While we doubt there will be many of us who will remember all of the figures for the dimensions of the cosmic alignment, we hope the camaraderie and friendships we each have experienced here will remain in our minds and hearts forever." Tomoiya side-eyed her friend.

"Whether you've made friendships or fallen in love," Moira started, her eyes lingering on the face of her boyfriend during a slight pause, "these are the people who you'll find yourself engaging in the years to come on one level or another. Please take a moment to glance around at each other's faces so that in times of trouble or adversity, you can think back and remember them as they are right now."

"We hope when you do encounter each other once again outside these walls, it is these faces, representing the joy and happiness you shared together, that will come to mind," Tomoiya continued. "We've been taught how to solve problems without violence - how to co-exist despite differences. As each of you move into a position of power, think back to those lessons. We are the future. We can make a difference. Through each of you, the Universe can be a better place. Homelessness, poverty, murder and war - if none of them existed, imagine how much better life would be. Together we have the power to make them meaningless words."

"Go forth and strive for greatness!" Moira yelled, tossing her flat red cap in the air, followed by an explosion of applause mixed with expressions of happiness.

Tomoiya stood still, not wanting to move. Her eyes glossed over, watching hundreds of red caps floating down to the ground. If she could freeze moments in time forever, that would have been one of them. The sides of her mouth curled upwards feeling the arms of her best friend wrapped around her shoulders.

"We did it!" Moira whispered, grabbing the cap still perched on Tomoiya's head and tossing it high in the air.

"Hey!" Tomoiya screamed. Her hands covered her head.

"You look beautiful, as always," Moira said, rolling her eyes.

"You mean plain, as always," Tomoiya barked back. "Although, the state of my hair is bound to draw extra attention."

"I don't know why you do that," Moira said. "You are absolutely gorgeous. You have confidence about everything else, why not your looks?"

"You're biased," Tomoiya answered. "Best friends don't count. I think they fall into the same category as mothers and fathers."

Moira giggled. "I'm not the only one who thinks you are a catch. Mick has been chasing you since the day you met him. I don't know why you won't go out with him."

"Not this again," Tomoiya said, picking up her cap. The gold tassel danced between her fingers. "You know why - my father would never allow me to date anyone."

"What your father doesn't know, isn't going to hurt him," Moira said.

"He knows all," Tomoiya replied, her eyelids opening to their fullest point. "Besides, I don't actually like Mick that way."

"What's not to like?" Moira asked. "He's fun, well-spoken and popular. All that and he's good-looking. If I wasn't already dating his best friend I might think about it."

Tomoiya sighed. "I don't know." She often wondered how Mick was enrolled in their school. He wasn't royalty, or even rich. In fact, he was rather ordinary. For some reason, when he spoke, people listened - hanging on every word. That was rather creepy, in her opinion.

4

"Think of it this way," Moira said. "If I marry Fallin and you marry Mick, we'd be able to be together forever."

"Do we really need men to stay friends?" Tomoiya asked. "I'd hope we could handle that on our own."

"It was worth a shot," Moira said, smiling. "Let's get some pictures taken and grab something to eat."

"I'm starving," Tomoiya admitted. "Let's skip the pictures."

The Royal Institution they attended was made for convenience. It consisted of one entire solar system, which had been terraformed to specific needs: a planet for classes; a planet for students who required residence; a planet for restaurants and shopping; and a planet for relaxation with beaches and spas. Within that cluster, everything and anything one might consider essential could be found.

"No way," Moira replied. "I want pictures and lots of them."

Giggling.

Chapter Two

"Don't think you ladies can break your diets just because school is over," Fallin said, squishing into the booth seat. He slid his arm around Moira in the same motion.

Smooth moves - confident or needy.

"What is that supposed to mean?" Tomoiya asked.

"It means," Mick answered, sliding in the seat beside her, "he wants his girl to keep her great figure."

Tomoiya coughed. The bluntness of his words, combined with a certain lack of emotion in his voice, caught her off-guard.

"Let's face it," Mick continued, ignoring the fry that Moira hurled at him, "just because high school is over, doesn't mean you girls need to let it all go. Ow!"

A high five across the table between the girls was well-deserved. Tomoiya had landed an impressive punch that was bound to leave a mark.

Bruises fade away - their lessons once learned, forgotten as easily as the mark that disappeared.

Fallin laughed. "You asked for it," he said. "By the way, I thought you ladies did a fabulous job as co-valedictorians. That speech was amazing."

"Yeah," Mick agreed. "Way to implant a political agenda in the minds of unsuspecting young men and women."

"What?!" Tomoiya screamed, gathering the attention of the whole restaurant.

"You heard me," Mick replied. "Your message of peace and love was received by all. For a moment, I thought I was attending one of your fundraisers." The white table became a canvas for two stick figures born from a squeeze bottle of yellow mustard. He smiled at his creation as if it were a great work of art. He quickly added a red heart inscribed *Mick & Tomi.*

"Shut up, Mick," Moira demanded. "Why can't we want everyone to be as happy as we are?"

"You can want it as much as you like," Mick said. "That doesn't mean it's going to happen. The sooner you girls understand there are some real monsters out there, the better. Not everyone can be negotiated with, nor would you want to try."

"You mean like you?" Tomoiya asked.

Mick laughed. "Say what you will, my dear, but I have made it my mission to weed the monsters out of my life. That's how I plan to make the Universe a better place for my friends and family." Strands of her brown hair fell through his fingers.

"Hey!" she cried, leaning as far away from him as possible. Realizing there wasn't a lot of room to move in the booth, she gave up squiggling.

Monsters - a tricky word. What defined it? In a universe filled with diverse beings, those unknown had somehow been lumped into that category. Did anyone have the right to take away another person's happiness for simply being different?

In the end, it was really a matter of perspective - after all, all sentient life had one. If one considered a beautiful soaring bird from the eyes of a mouse, it became a monster.

Could a common ground ever exist?

"Galaxy to Tomoiya," Moira said, waving a hand in front of her face. "Hello." Her nose scrunched up as a pink tongue darted out between her lips.

"What?" Tomoiya answered. "Sorry."

"Where did you go?" Fallin chuckled.

"Daydreaming about me?" Mick asked, nudging her with his elbow.

"No!" Tomoiya exclaimed. "I was thinking, that's all. What did I miss other than the ridiculous face you made?"

"We were discussing the party tomorrow night," Moira responded. "You are planning on coming, aren't you?"

"Probably," Tomoiya muttered.

"Oh, come on," Moira whined. "This is one last blast when everyone will be together."

"Speaking of which," Mick interrupted, "did your father tell you which college he enrolled you in yet?"

Tomoiya sighed. "Not yet. The way things are going, I'll probably wake up one day to my bags packed and be sent without knowing to where."

"Why does he do that?" Fallin asked. "I don't know why you put up with it. Try rebelling once in a while. No princess was ever excommunicated for wanting a little freedom."

"He's only trying to keep me safe," Tomoiya answered. "Since my mother passed away, I'm all he has left."

"I get it," Mick said. "Albeit, sometimes being overprotective is as dangerous as not having any protection at all. What if you needed help? How could you get in touch with me?"

Fallin spit a mouthful of water across the table.

"Ew!" Moira screamed.

"What was that for?!" Mick yelled.

"Sorry," Fallin answered. "You sounded like you actually believed Tomoiya would call you first if she was in trouble. Dude, you aren't anywhere near the top of that list."

Laughter.

Chapter Three

Tomoiya glanced at her image in the full-length mirror, examining every angle possible. She looked as good as could be expected. No matter how many times people told her she was attractive, she couldn't see it. There was always something that didn't seem quite right about the person that reflected back at her. It lacked luster - it lacked life.

How could anyone truly be thought of as beautiful when their true self remained hidden?

She pulled on the bottom of her skirt, trying to lengthen it a smidgen. It had no effect. Back to the drawing board, or in her case a room-sized closet, to pick out a new outfit to try on. She settled on a white sun dress. The whole process of mirror examination began again. It was better, but not perfect. Nothing could ever be perfect in a Universe that made whole races hide in fear of discrimination.

Prejudice - the single most deadly term in existence. It caused more harm than natural disasters and created more wars than any other cause.

It became even more frightening when one considered how easily it spread, coupled with how impossible it was to control once it started.

She bounced once after flopping back on her oversized bed. Looking around her room, it was filled with constant reminders of how different she was. Teddy bears in all shapes and sizes sat on every dresser and shelf. Larger versions of the stuffed toy were propped up against walls. Some were adorned with pretty bows and dresses, while others remained plain. They came in all different colours and hailed from the far reaches of every corner of the Universe. One thing they all had in common, each one looked fluffy - not a regular fluffy, but the sort of furry softness that demanded a hugging.

Looks were deceiving.

Of course, each one had a purpose. Inside their furry exterior lay a hidden pocket filled with the sharpest items that ever existed - her tears. That was their job - their reason for existing - to do nothing more than collect her tears year after year. Each one did it well. By looking at them, it was impossible to guess a treasure beyond imagination was hidden inside each of their soft bellies.

Tomoiya reached behind her for the one bear that was allowed on her bed. It was the first of its kind and reflected its age. She caressed the battle scars that had accumulated during its long term of service as she gave it a once-over, looking for any new signs of wear and tear. Luckily, there wasn't anything she hadn't noticed before. The bear was holding together as well as could be expected considering its nose had been reattached several times and checkered patches that matched the pattern on the bottom of its feet had been sewn over spots where fur had worn thin.

12

She squeezed its belly then hugged it, not caring about the cargo hidden deep within.

Memories - they faded in and out without warning - more an involuntary response than a choice consciously made. Where did they go when they weren't being thought of?

*****

Memories...

An overwhelming scent of sickly sweet flowers filled her senses, making her want to vomit. From the smallest bud to a fully blooming flower taller than her guards, they were everywhere in the room, but especially concentrated around where her mother lay. Any other day, she would have enjoyed examining each - their colours - their designs. The Universe fascinated her. She wanted to see new places - to explore how different things were from one place to another. To her culture told a story greater than any fairytale.

Today, however, was different. She didn't know how or why, but something inside felt wrong.

Intuition - even the youngest child had experienced it - perhaps, it was something all born had. One could argue that every species was given it, in one form or another - a common thread whose job it has always been to create a link between all life.

Tomoiya was only just tall enough to see her mother's perfect porcelain white skin and dark hair. Her eyelids remained closed and motionless. Everything seemed surreal: her life; her surroundings - all clouded over as if shrouded in a mist - a fog that wasn't real.

Emotions - when strong enough, perhaps they could be seen; their presence sensed in the physical world.

"Why can't I talk to her?" Tomoiya asked.

"You can," her father answered. "She just can't answer the way she used to." He squatted down beside her. After nodding to his guards to leave, he continued. "Your mother has gone to another place. You have to feel her answers in here." He pointed to her chest.

"But I can see her. She is lying right there!" Tomoiya exclaimed.

He turned his daughter's body to face his. "That looks like your mother, but she isn't there anymore. I know this is hard for you to understand."

"Can I go with her?" Tomoiya asked.

"One day," he answered. "But not until it's your turn to leave this dimension. That won't be for a very long time."

"But I want to see her," Tomoiya cried, pain stinging her eyes - tears begging for release.

"Do you remember the rules she taught you?" he questioned.

"Yes," Tomoiya admitted.

"What was number one?"

"A princess never cries in public," Tomoiya answered.

"Very good," her father praised. "That one is especially important for you. Do you know why?"

Tomoiya shook her head, her body joining in the motion.

"It's because your tears are too precious to ever give anyone. No one has the right to make my perfect little girl cry."

"How do I stop from being sad?" Tomoiya asked.

14

"I don't expect you to," her father answered. "There will be times in your life when you will be sad." He reached into the pocket inside his black suit and removed a light brown bear. "This little guy is going to be your friend and help you."

"How?" she asked.

"When you are sad, take him with you to a place where you are all alone. He'll listen to all your problems and, if you need to cry, he'll collect your tears." He flipped the bear over and pushed the fur on his back to the side revealing a tiny zipper.

"What happens if he gets full?" She asked.

"He'll invite a friend to come and help." His lips brushed the top of her forehead. "But hopefully you won't have so many tears it will come to that."

"What if he runs out of friends?" Tomoiya asked.

He smiled. "My dear Tomoiya, one day someone will give you the last teddy bear you ever need. That person will make sure you are so happy you will never have to shed another tear." His hand gently caressed the side of her face. "Trust me. It may not seem like it, but that day will come."

*****

Tomoiya sighed. That day hadn't come yet. She glanced down at the funny face of the bear in her hands and chuckled. She flipped him over and unzipped the secret compartment. A few dozen tear-shaped golden diamonds fell out. Somehow, the other toys never felt right as her confidant. They had taken on the role of guardians instead. She carried

15

the handful of gems over to one of the larger bears resting on the floor and their new home. In her mind, only the original could be the collector.

She glanced at her image in the mirror one more time, the bear still clenched in one hand tightly. It would have to do. There wasn't anyone she wanted to impress that evening anyways. She already knew she'd be stuck with Mick following her around like a lost puppy. She chuckled. If he had actually been a puppy, she might have liked him more.

She replaced her bear on the bed to faithfully wait for her return. Moira was right. Tonight would be the last time she would see many of the friends she had made in high school. Odds were, they would never all be together in the same place again. Tonight was about celebrating friendships.

Chapter Four

"You look amazing!" Moira exclaimed.

The door to the shuttle squeaked closed. She glanced over her shoulder at it. "Mick should get that fixed," Tomoiya said, "or get a new one. I'm surprised my father let me leave in it."

"Don't be so negative," Moira pouted. "He was nice enough to send it for you. Not many guys are that considerate nowadays. Chivalry is on its way out. When you see him, you should thank him for the gesture rather than insulting his equipment."

"You do know how wrong that sounded, don't you?" Tomoiya said, unable to hold back a giggle. "Where are those two anyways?"

"I don't know," Moira replied. "They'll find us later on the beach. We should build a sand castle like before." She linked her arm with Tomoiya's. It was a normal position for the two. Other students rarely batted an eye at them being joined at the waist, walking somewhere together.

"Let's!" Tomoiya agreed.

Mirage-Three was the most popular destination in the high school owned galaxy. There, the sun and moon having equal strength in light and heat made round-the-clock sandy beaches a teenage dream resort. Only twice a year the planet experienced any darkness at all. That evening was one of those nights. In those rare occurrences, the moon would completely vanish from the sky for approximately four hours.

Magic made everyday life extraordinary.

The walk from space port to beach was only steps. In fact, the walk from anywhere to a beach was only steps. It was a picture-perfect paradise. Once off of the pavement, it took mere seconds for Tomoiya to shed her shoes, letting the warm sand move between her wiggling toes.

"That feels amazing," she said, smiling. "I swear this sand is softer than anywhere else I've been."

"It is," Moira agreed. "Over there." She pointed to a section of beach that had been roped off.

"Did you do that?"

"Nope," Moira answered. "The guys did. Need a pail?"

Tomoiya took the plastic play set her friend offered. "You thought of everything." It was only the third time the girls had been on the sand to witness the effects of darkness in a place that never goes dark.

Moira held up a small rock. "Do you think this one will work?" she asked, examining it from every side.

"It looks good," Tomoiya answered. "Can you tell what colour it will be?"

18

"Pink, I think. I never was good at guessing," Moira said. "Maybe I can figure it out today."

Tomoiya picked up a similar stone and held it up to the sun. Barely visible, tiny specs of blue lit up and faded as the pebble turned in between two fingers.

"Do you want to use the same colour scheme?" Moira asked.

"Uh-huh," Tomoiya answered, examining another stone. "Pink for windows, blue for the moat, orange for fireplaces and green for doors. I'll grab the water. You can start digging."

The bucket disappeared under the water surface with only a tiny bit of the green plastic left visible. It was strange to think the crystal clear water she was wading through had the potential to be dangerous. It was almost the perfect trap. Her feet rejoiced at the cool refreshing sensation of the ocean making the rest of her body jealous. Swimming at the beach, however, was strictly on a *use at your own risk* basis.

Rule number fifty-five - a princess, whenever possible, avoided taking unnecessary risks.

The first time she met Moira had been in that very spot. She was a naive young girl attending school for the first time. Moira caught her off-guard, making her believe magic swooshed away anything that became submerged under the water's surface. That, of course, wasn't true. It was a natural illusion. Anything under the water was merely hidden from sight. Still, it took her a full year to figure out the truth.

Two boys splashing well outside the safety lines caught her attention. She shook her head. That was a bit too dangerous for her. Swimming was one thing, but not knowing what was swimming beside you was another.

It was impossible to prepare for a problem which didn't appear to exist.

She ran back to shore, carefully ducking under the rope so as not to spill the bucket's much-needed cargo.

"Nice moat," Tomoiya said. "It's a little large though, isn't it? I think several families could occupy that big a place."

"Going big!" Moira squealed, tossing sand in the air.

Laughter.

Within minutes, their castle began to take form. Moira carefully placed pebbles in the moat, situating a few stragglers in such a way as to light up the only bridge crossing over. "This is going to be so amazing. I can't wait to see it finished."

"It is," Tomoiya agreed, carefully carving out windows and placing the tiny sand flecks inside. "How long do you think we have?"

"Not long," Moira answered, nodding at a shadow that had already started creeping towards them. "I'm going to miss this."

"Building sand castles?" Tomoiya asked, crinkling up her nose. "I'm sure you can come back anytime you want to. I doubt the school will deny its past student body entry."

"No, silly," Moira replied. "You - I'm going to miss you." A handful of sand slid through her fingers to the ground. "You're the best friend I have ever had. I don't know what I'll do without you. What happens when I don't see you every day? I tell you just about everything."

"Just about?" Tomoiya asked, side-eyeing her friend. A coy smile graced her lips.

"Yeah," Moira admitted. "I want time to be able to tell you so much more. I want things to stay like today forever. I want us to stay this way."

There was an honesty in her words that hit home. "I do too," Tomoiya said, swallowing back a mouthful of saliva. That was the truth. More than anything she wished she could share her deepest secrets with her best friend, but it wasn't possible. Anonymity wasn't a choice, but rather a requirement.

Guilt - It was unavoidable for anyone with a conscience.

"Why do things have to change?"

"I don't know," Tomoiya answered. "Maybe because the Universe never stops evolving. We adapt or disappear."

"Wow, that got dark fast," Moira commented.

"Almost as fast as it's gonna get dark here in a few minutes," Tomoiya stated.

Excitement returned to Moira's eyes. "You're right," she said. "Here it comes."

Chapter Five

"Ladies," Mick said. "Great job on the sand castle." He glanced over his shoulder at the shadows closing in fast. "What are you pointing at?"

"Nothing," Moira said. "Here. Take our picture when it lights up."

For a split-second, the ocean surface burnt hues of red and orange - a sea of fire set ablaze by a celestial god. Albeit, the scene was merely reflection, it was still enough to send shivers running up and down Tomoiya's spine.

Experiencing the momentary change in the moon's colour before it disappeared from the horizon was something she would never forget. As quick as it started, it was over - as if in one single second all the light of the moon burnt into oblivion, leaving only darkness in its place.

The tiny pebbles began to work their magic. Each one had the unique ability to hold minuscule amounts of energy collected from light sources. As soon as that source extinguished, the stored power was released. The result - an illumination of the natural colours the fragments contained.

A stunning blue moat appeared surrounding the sand castle. Inside the structure, windows lit up as if someone flipped a switch. Pink shadows cast on a white background provided an illusion of a tiny fairy family living inside.

"It's perfect," Moira said, clapping her hands together and jumping up and down.

Tomoiya knelt on the opposite side of the sandy building from her best friend. A couple of clicks and the moment was preserved forever.

Time - an unmeasurable amount of singular moments happening in different places simultaneously, each one unique, deserving to be treasured. While time could be preserved, once past, it could never be relived.

"You ladies outdid yourselves," Mick said, pointing a camera in their direction.

"What are you doing?" Moira asked.

"I am capturing everything that happens tonight in movie magic," he answered.

"Stop messing around," Moira demanded, knocking the camera away from her face.

"Don't you want to be a star?" Mick mused. "You two are in the leading roles."

"Where's Fallin?" Moira asked, turning her attention back to adding more colour to the sand castle.

"I'm glad you asked!" Mick exclaimed, kicking the side of the castle. The walls caved in and it tumbled down, reverting back to a mere pile of dirt.

"What did you do that for?!" Moira screamed.

"It served its purpose," Mick explained, laughing. "You girls had fun building it. I preserved the moment for you in a picture, then I had fun knocking it down. It's a win-win - everybody is happy."

"I'm not sure I am," Tomoiya muttered.

"Don't be silly," Mick said. "It wasn't going to last forever anyways. One wind storm and nothing would have been left. This way you got to share a bit of the fun with me."

Could logic that was not logical but still made sense be argued with?

"What exactly does this have to do with Fallin?" Moira asked, crossing her arms over her chest.

"I am supposed to bring you ladies to him," he answered. "He has a surprise for you. If you will follow me, my dear - to where your story began." He bowed with one hand behind his back. The other outstretched in front of him, indicating the direction they were heading in.

Tomoiya's usual stride made it difficult to keep up, even though her legs were considerably longer than Moira's. "Where is he taking us?" she whispered, picking up her pace to match her friend's.

Moira's face beamed brighter than the pebbles. "I think we are going to the alcove where I first met Fallin," she explained.

Up until then, Tomoiya had never understood the meaning of the saying *a larger than life grin.* Looking at her friend at that exact moment, it all made sense. It was an expression of the single happiest time in a person's life and it was contagious. Their arms intertwined.

Mick side-eyed the girls. "Wow, you two did a complete one-eighty. I can barely tell where one smile starts and the other ends. You know, you are supposed to wait to find out what the surprise is before you get excited."

Laughter.

Chapter Six

"Why didn't I notice this before?" Tomoiya asked, examining the almost private beach neatly tucked away between the jagged red rocks and clay that made up a surrounding cliff.

"It's strange," Moira answered. "The whole place is only visible in the dark. I'm not sure why, but unless you know exactly where it is, you'll never find it in the light."

"How did you find it?"

"I saw this cute guy disappear one day," Moira explained. "Naturally, I followed. What else was a girl to do?"

Tomoiya chuckled. With everything the two talked about, there were still things she didn't know about her best friend. "So that's how you two met," she said. Of course, she felt a little silly for not asking sooner.

"It was," Moira admitted. "I actually got lost and couldn't find my way back out. Fallin saved me." She used her hand to mimic an old-fashioned fan in motion.

"She faked being lost, if you ask me," Mick said, pushing past the two girls. "Come on. Lover boy is waiting. Don't forget to smile for the camera."

"Are you seriously planning on keeping that thing recording all night?" Tomoiya asked.

Mick stopped and aimed the camera at her. "I am," he said. "Give me a smile, beautiful."

"It would help if you were aiming it at her face and not her legs," Moira pointed out.

Mick laughed. "Can't blame a guy for hoping for a big gust of wind. These beaches are known for some strong and unexpected blasts."

Tomoiya gasped. Her hands dropped down to flatten her dress. An instinctual movement as there wasn't even a hint of a breeze.

"You're safe, Princess," he said. "At least for now." He fired off a wink in her direction. "I'm going to run ahead to capture you two coming in." He disappeared behind a boulder.

"What do you think this is all about?" Tomoiya asked.

"Your guess is as good as mine," Moira answered. "Fallin didn't mention a word to me about it."

"Wow!" Tomoiya exclaimed. Grabbing Moira's shoulders, she turned her friend to take in the view.

It was the most beautiful thing Tomoiya had ever seen an individual do for another person. Her gaze froze - locked staring at a gigantic heart made entirely out of reflecting pebbles. It must have taken days to find enough red to form the outline - not to mention the thousands of pink needed to fill it in.

Moira ran forward, throwing her arms around Fallin's neck. "You romantic jerk!" she cried. "I love it." Tears ran down the sides of her face.

A princess never cried in public - even from joy. All emotions remained hidden at all costs.

Tomoiya widened her eyes, trying to alleviate the stinging sensation she knew accompanied the forming of tears.

Distraction changed emotions.

She focused her attention on the couple in front of her - or more importantly, the extreme differences between two.

Fallin was the tallest person she knew, standing a full head and shoulders over all the other boys at the school, including Mick. He had long, wavy, dark hair, which he kept messily tied back in a bun. That, coupled with his muscular build, drew every girl's attention. His eyes, however, were always on Moira. Although he was quick to rough-house with the boys, when he was with her, he was a gentle giant.

Moira, on the other hand, could be described as petite and dainty. If one didn't know them and saw the two from a distance, one might have thought she was his child.

"Not going to cry, are you?" Mick asked.

Good old Mick to the rescue. He always knew what not to say and blurted it out anyways. That was exactly the distraction she needed to regain complete control. As a reward, she did what she always did - punched him in the shoulder. Her confidence that he expected the blow translated into force.

"Ow!" he yelled. "What did I do?"

"Nothing," she answered, smiling. "Shouldn't you be capturing this moment for your movie?"

"I was until you hit me," he whined, frowning.

"I thought you were a tough guy," she teased.

"If you two are done arguing," Fallin interrupted, "I'd like you to be witnesses."

"Witnesses?" Moira asked.

Fallin placed a finger over Moira's cherry coloured lips. "Sh." A playfulness danced in his eyes as they glanced over his girlfriend from head to toe. He soaked in every bit of her radiance and reflected it back in his movements.

Tomoiya always envied her friend's appearance. Moira was anything but ordinary. Her red, curly hair was always perfect - not a strand out of place. Even in a rain storm, those ringlets would bounce right back up into their perky forms, reminding her of soldiers lining up for attention at roll call.

Military life - once learnt, never forgotten. Rule one hundred and one - a princess needed to possess the ability to protect herself if necessary.

Fallin took one of Moira's dainty hands into one of his own. He dropped to one knee and held out a beautiful ring. "Marry me." His words sung promises of forever.

Moira gasped, her free hand covering her mouth. She inhaled deeply a few times before blurting out, "Yes!" As if that one word took everything to say, she fell on her knees and into his arms. The two embraced.

Love - it was thought to conquer all; a magic stronger than any other form - meant to be everlasting.

"I got it all!" Mick yelled, ruining the moment. "You are going to love the way this mush translates onto the big screen."

"Thanks," Fallin said, helping his bride-to-be to her feet. He slapped Mick on the back. The two engaged in what could only be described as a primal male contest of strength - or wrestling. A few grunts later and the sappy moment was gone, buried deep within mounds of pure testosterone.

Tomoiya threw her arms around Moira from behind. "Congratulations! I am so happy for you."

"Thanks," Moira replied, her hand reaching up to meet Tomoiya's.

That one touch spoke a thousand words. There was something wrong. There was happiness, but something was missing.

When putting together a puzzle, being able to recognize the final picture wasn't enough. One missing piece tended to ruin the end result.

"Are you okay?"

"Tomoiya," Moira whispered, "I have a secret."

"What?"

"I..."

"You two ladies ready to head to the party?!" Mick yelled over, starting to film again.

"We'll be right there!" Moira hollered back.

"Wait," Tomoiya said, grabbing her arm. "You were going to say something important."

Moira smiled. If there had been something wrong, it certainly wasn't showing now. "I'll tell you tomorrow. I really should talk to Fallin first anyways. I'm getting married!" A high-pitched squeal followed her words.

"Are you sure?" Tomoiya asked.

"Yeah," Moira answered. "I want to have fun tonight. It's not like either of us are going anywhere before the morning. Maybe I can stay over. There is a lot I'd like to tell you." Happiness faded into complacency.

"Sounds good." Tomoiya agreed. Her home was nearly always empty except for guards and staff. A sleepover sounded perfect.

A secret - maybe everyone had one. Maybe that was life's meaning - learning which secrets to keep and which to share.

The boys were well in the lead and showed no signs of slowing down. Tomoiya quickened her step, not wanting to be left behind. Watching them walk, it occurred to her for the first time that they were little more than strangers. Other than the fact that Mick and Fallin had known each other since birth and their families had been friends for generations, she really didn't know much else about either one. Shouldn't she know more about her closest friends? Maybe they had secrets too.

Where did intuition end and paranoia begin? Trust needed to be the basis for all relationships.

Chapter Seven

Tomoiya shook her head at a group of boys attempting to juggle lit torches near the water's edge. Every now and then, a piece of clothing caught on fire and someone yelled, "Stop! Drop! And Roll!" over top of a constant chanting of the word *chug* in the background. This wasn't one of the civilized parties she was used to attending. Still, there was something appealing about it.

Rule thirty-one - a princess must never be seen in inappropriate surroundings or engaging in questionable activities.

She looked around and realized Mick was nowhere to be seen. They must have separated in the crowd - a welcome break. Moira and Fallin had disappeared as soon as they hit the party, leaving her alone with him. It wasn't that she disliked Mick, but all the talk about dating and love was sometimes a bit much. Besides, she needed a chance to catch up with a few other friends she might not see again for a very long time.

"Tomoiya!" A girl yelled, running towards her - not exactly one of the people she was expecting or hoping to run into.

A glow-in-the-dark florescent liquid splashed over top of the rim of a plastic cup firmly gripped in one hand. The girl either didn't notice or didn't care. Drinks were easily replaced in any number of spots.

"Hi," Tomoiya said, trying to remember the girl's name. She was sure it started with an L. They had taken one course together this past year, albeit Tomoiya couldn't remember ever speaking to her directly.

"It's me, Lizelle," she said.

That was it, Lizelle. At least she had the L part right. "Ancient languages," Tomoiya said, holding her cup up for a cheers and to block an oncoming hug. Their two cups bashed together - more liquid went flying. She managed to side-step the bulk of it.

"Isn't this amazing?!" Lizelle exclaimed. "Good friends all together being happy - makes me happy."

Tomoiya smiled and nodded. It didn't take a genius to realize the girl had consumed one too many drinks. There was something in her words, as jumbled as they were, that hit a nerve.

Friends - what was it that qualified someone to be called one? Surely just knowing a person wasn't enough.

Did Lizelle really consider her a friend? She didn't know the first thing about the girl and was pretty sure Lizelle didn't know the first thing about her. But then she didn't know that much about Mick and Fallin either or, for that matter, Moira. Sure, they spent a lot of time together and she knew what each of them would order at a restaurant, but details were missing. There had to be more.

"Oh," Lizelle said. "I almost forgot. Mick has been looking for you. You are so lucky to have a catch like him. I wish I was you."

The sound of his name brought her back from her thoughts. She wasn't sure how to answer. Luckily, she didn't have to.

"You need a new drink!" Lizelle yelled, grabbing her arm and dragging her to the nearest makeshift bar. "Here." A plastic cup slammed into Tomoiya's hand. "Can't have a good time without a few of these."

Rule number thirty-three - a princess never overindulged in public. That included food; alcohol; and emotions.

"Hi, Lizelle," another girl said. This one Tomoiya didn't recognize, partly she assumed do to the amount of makeup that was slathered all over her face.

"Hi," Lizelle answered, spilling more of her drink. "This is my best friend, Tomoiya." She threw an arm around Tomoiya's shoulders, luckily it was the one not attached to a drink.

Could strangers really be best friends?

Tomoiya smiled and nodded a hello, hoping that would be enough to satisfy her newfound besties. The band warming up saved her from any further interaction. *Interstellar Perfection* was the hottest group in the Universe. Someone spared no expense getting them to appear. Who and why didn't seem to matter to anyone else.

Screams.

Fans exploded with emotions for performers they had never met. Tomoiya gasped as personalities morphed before her eyes. Individuals who were normally calm and collected became wild and unruly. It was as

35

if they were running for their lives, knocking each other down without caring. Compassion went out the window.

The future leaders of the Universe not willing or able to cooperate with one another at a concert, yet expected to rule.

The area directly in front of the band filled quickly with screaming girls pushing and shoving for positions. The stage itself was bombarded with love letters mixed in with some undergarments meant to be tokens of dedication and emotion.

Love - was it really that easy to feel?

Royalty willing to do anything to prove their undying love for musicians they had never met.

Music had always been thought of as an expression of one's self. Was it possible to know someone simply by listening to their music?

It wasn't a concept that she couldn't easily grasp. To be honest, outside of family, she had never felt any emotion for another individual, at least not one strong enough to make her gush over them. Maybe she wasn't normal, but her underwear was staying where it belonged.

Was history the norm or the masses going against what once was? A standard had to be set somehow.

"Crazy, isn't it," Mick said, sneaking up behind her.

Tomoiya jumped, dropping her cup. That offered a bit of relief - she didn't have to pretend to drink it anymore.

"I totally got that on film," Mick smirked. "You should have seen your face. It's priceless. Ow!"

Tomoiya's usual punch landed in the same spot as always. She sighed. "I'm actually not all that disturbed to have found you."

"Who found who?" Mick asked, circling her, the camera still capturing everything.

"Lizelle said you were looking for me," she continued, ignoring his question.

"Lizelle?" Mick echoed. "I didn't know you knew each other. Regardless, I never asked her about you. She must have overheard me talking with someone else."

"That actually makes a lot of sense," Tomoiya admitted. "Apparently, she considers me her best friend. I don't think we've talked more than once before today."

Mick snorted out his beer. "She isn't royalty."

Neither are you, Tomoiya thought. She didn't have the nerve to say it out loud. Truth or not, people treated Mick as if he were a pure-blood royal. There was simply something about him that demanded that level of respect, warranted or not. Her father called it *the gift of the gab.*

Well placed words in the wrong hands have always been deadlier than any weapon.

"Have you gotten everything you wanted recorded?" she asked, changing the topic.

"And then some," Mick said.

She was lucky to catch all three words. The band had begun its first song, *Conquering Hearts Bleed Tonight.* Within seconds, Mick was screaming the lyrics along with them.

"Let's get closer for a better picture!" he yelled in her ear.

Before she had a chance to answer, he was dragging her through the crowd towards the band shell. She hadn't expected him to be allowed backstage, but then she always seemed to underestimate the things he did.

Mick motioned with one finger and mouthed the word *stay*. A few moments later he returned with a chair. Without allowing her a chance to refuse, he ushered her onto the stage.

Put on a pedestal like an object - meant to be adored, but not move... or think. Such admiration borderlined on confinement or imprisonment.

In this atmosphere, the wooden chair was as grand as any throne. Those girls who weren't already envious of the attention Mick gave her, definitely hated her after that. The good part, she didn't have to see them at school again. In time they would forget tonight - or not...

The lead singer dropped to one knee in front of her. Taking one hand in his own, he sang to her as if she was the only female left alive. Red crept into her cheeks. She wasn't swooning over him as much as she was embarrassed.

"Do you like it?" Mick asked, using a microphone - the music still playing in the background. "I had them come and sing especially for you. I want you to know I need you in my life."

Her heart raced. She wasn't sure what was happening. One thing she did know, this was something no one on the beach would easily forget. There was a chance the moment might even haunt her forever.

Haunt was the right word, but for the reason unanticipated.

Mick dropped to one knee in front of her chair. "Tomoiya..."

A lump formed in her throat. He couldn't be proposing. They had never even dated. Her father would never allow this.

Panic - totally irrational and completely uncontrollable.

38

She pulled him closer to her. "Wait," she whispered, pulling the microphone away from their faces. She looked out into the crowd - his friend filming every moment. "My father..."

"Don't worry," he interrupted. "I am working on something important. When I get final authorization, your father will beg me to marry you. We will be together no matter what. That, I promise you." He slid a ring onto her shaking finger.

"What..."

"Sh," he whispered. Standing, Mick faced the crowd. "She accepted!" he announced.

More than anything, she hadn't wanted any confrontation tonight. This evening was supposed to be about friends and fun. Arguing now would merely ruin the celebration for everyone else. It was definitely a better idea to break it off later, without such a large audience. Of course, she couldn't let him know he was off the hook. She smiled and took his hand.

"That wasn't fair," she whispered, a crocodile smile plastered to her face. "We'll discuss this later."

He brushed his lips against her cheeks, completely unaffected by her words. "In private, I hope."

She sighed. Of course he had taken her words the wrong way. In the background, the song ended. After shaking the hands of each of the band members, she moved towards the stairs. A series of shrill-screams stopped her in her tracks.

Only tragedy had the ability to silence a crowd.

The screams became louder - moving closer. Tomoiya leaned towards Mick. She didn't need to be in love with him to trust him enough to protect her. The noises were deafening. Something was being tortured. It was a sound like none she had heard before.

As she anticipated, Mick pushed her behind him. Although she had training in both defence and combat, she was at a disadvantage not being able to take her natural form in public.

The crowd remained silent as it parted. With everyone trying to peek at what was coming their way, Tomoiya couldn't make out the figures until they were directly below.

Disbelief.

Her heart raced. "What are you doing?" she screamed, leaping forward.

Mick pushed her back hard enough to knock her over. "Fallin!" he yelled, motioning with one hand for Tomoiya to remain on her rump.

"She's one of them, Mick!" Fallin cried. "She's a fucking vampire." He motioned to Moira's limp body behind him.

Tomoiya screamed at her first full glimpse of her friend. It was worse than she originally thought. The sight of blood and exposed scalp where hair had been pulled out made her nauseous. Even without taking a single sip of alcohol all night, she still felt the lightheadedness that normally was associated with drinking heavily. If she hadn't already been on the ground, there was no doubt she would have fallen over.

Questions filled her mind. *How far had he dragged her by her hair? How could he do this to the woman he loved and was going to marry?* Her gaze met Moira's. She gasped at the new colour of her best friend's eyes - a crystallized green.

"Please help me!" Moira screamed, fang-like teeth exposed for the world to see. Her inner-self standing trial alone for the crimes of an entire species - crimes that never existed.

A Vampire Pledge - To protect our kind, one's true self may never be shown to those unable or unwilling to understand and accept.

Tomoiya froze. There was no doubt, Moira was a vampire. But, why wasn't she fighting back? Or trying to escape?

"I used the stuff," Fallin said, tossing her into the crowd. "It works. She can't move from the shoulders down." He kicked her midsection with full force. "Do you like that?"

Moira screamed. Pain radiated from her direction like an aura, yet her body remained still.

"It can feel everything," Fallin continued without emotion.

Tomoiya jutted forward a second time, only to be pulled back. "She's my friend!" she cried.

"That isn't Moira anymore," Mick explained.

He turned to face hundreds of eyes searching for answers. They needed an explanation - validation. Mick, being who he was, wouldn't disappoint.

"That isn't Moira anymore!" he yelled. "That is a beast who took over her body. A vampire!"

Mumbles.

"Far too long have these creatures been left to grow in numbers. Now, it's too late. They have infiltrated royalty and taken one of our own. My family predicted this day would come. No one listened, but now you will."

Fear enveloped all those it came in contact with. When its wheels began to turn, fate was sealed. A shadow, which once started, was impossible to stop.

"Take her further down the beach where we won't be affected by its evil gaze," Mick demanded. "I'll be there soon with further instructions. Don't be fooled by its lies, either. Treachery is in the nature of the beast."

"What should we do with her while we wait for you?" A blonde boy yelled back.

"Whatever you want," Fallin answered. "No one here cares what happens to a vampire."

Laughter of men given a license to torture.

Chapter Eight

"Don't move," Mick warned. "Things are going to change very fast now. You don't want to be labeled a monster supporter. Bloodthirsty people won't think twice about lumping supporters with offenders. Not even I could help you if that happens. Stay put and you'll be safe. Right now, your engagement to me is what is keeping you from being accused."

Guilty by association and exposed for everything that was. The innocent accused and damned without proof.

She froze, listening to the sound of her own breathing - shallow and irregular. A Plan. That was what she needed, but what? Her eyes searched the faces of those once considered her closest friends. Now, each one reminded her of Lizelle. There was no help in sight. Mick was her only chance to make it through the night.

Principles were often sacrificed for safety. A deal with a devil, once made, could never be broken.

She winced at the return of screams from further down the beach. Her mind wandered to the horrors her best friend was probably being subjected to. Her lips parted, words begging for release - wanting to yell out that Moira wasn't any different than before. A single glance from Mick was enough to silence her.

"Society buried the truth, but now with this undeniable proof, they won't be able to deny the need for Purifiers!" Mick exclaimed, taking centre stage. He was now the star of the film he had been making all evening. Perhaps that had always been his vision. "I come from the Purifier lineage! The ancestors of myself and my boys, fought these monsters to keep the universe safe. Society demanded the sacrifices my predecessors made be silenced. We will be muzzled no longer!"

His friends roared a cheer.

A butcher leading animals to slaughter - each one blind to the consequences of their own actions.

"Since the original Purifiers disbanded many generations ago, we have been rebuilding our ranks. We knew this day would come. We knew these creatures would return and someone needed to be ready!"

"You're the man, Mick!" Fallin yelled.

"We were lucky enough to still have records of the great battles fought long ago. That information is what led us to realize, in a one-on-one fight, man isn't the stronger of the two races."

A chorus of boos.

"Now. Now," Mick said, his hand outstretched in front of him, palms facing the crowd. "Don't worry. That's why we have been working

44

on some new weapons that will give us the advantage. The X3-IV66 drug, developed in our private laboratories, stops a vampire from being able to move from the shoulders down."

Cheers.

Mick laughed, exposing a few golden teeth. A detail that had escaped being noticed before.

Gold teeth - fake, yet expensive - like everything else about him.

"You haven't heard the best part, yet!" Mick yelled, the tone of his voice demanding further praise from the masses. "It isn't paralysis. These beasts can still feel everything we do to them. We can extract information with ease. But wait, that's not all. We managed to isolate what we call the monster gene. The X3-IV66 drug forces these beasts to show their real identity. There won't be any hiding among us anymore."

Rumbles.

"Are you going to use that crap on all of us as well?" A boy named Hoarani yelled from the crowd. Within seconds, he was on the ground bleeding and regretting each word.

"Do you have something to hide?" Fallin asked, standing over the latest victim of his previously latent brutality.

The gentle giant was slain and replaced by an angry one.

Hoarani cowered in Fallin's shadow, rolling himself into a ball to protect as much of his body as possible.

"Luckily," Mick said, jumping off the stage, "the drug doesn't affect our kind. It attacks only the monster gene, which those of us with nothing to hide don't have." He pulled a syringe out of a bag on Fallin's back. "Technically, we aren't cleared to test this on the general public. We do, however, have backing from enough worlds and religious leaders to test those individuals considered suspicious." He plunged the needle into Hoarani's arm. "Like you."

A few minutes passed in silenced. Hoarani moved his hands from his face to peek out. Whatever was in the syringe had no effect on him. The poor kid must have been holding his breath. It all came out in one giant huff.

"Hm," Mick said. "Guess you are one of us, after all." His hand reached down to help Hoarani to his feet. He chuckled. Of course, he wasn't the only one snickering at the noticeable wet spot between the boy's legs. "Sorry 'bout that. We needed to be sure." He smacked Hoarani's back. "Keep in mind, supporters are our enemies as well. Those willing to make deals with demons aren't our allies."

A demon by definition - one who acted as a tormentor within the boundaries of all that was considered evil. Where only one party endured torture, it begged to question, who was the victim?

"Now we have the testing we needed, it won't be long before the X3-IV66 drug goes into mass production!" Mick exclaimed.

Cheers.

Mick offered his hand. "Come," he demanded.

A mouse trapped in a maze, turned corner after corner, desperately searching for its freedom - always seeking and never finding. Such a life made for a poor existence.

Tomoiya's shaking hand found its way into his grip. She bit down on the inside of her bottom lip, forcing back tears demanding a teddy bear audience. The salty metallic taste of her own blood mixed with saliva.

Pain. When used correctly could be a useful distraction.

46

Mick reached up and grabbed her waist, pulling her down from the stage. "Stick close," he ordered. "My future bride needs to put in a good showing for me."

The race of man had become living walls - directing the mouse where they wanted it to be. The mouse complied out of either sheer stupidity or an instinctual desire for self-preservation. Either way, in the end there never was an exit waiting to be discovered.

Flanked on either side by Mick and Fallin, Tomoiya kept her gaze from meeting observers along the way. One glance back from Mick and the music began playing again, drowning out the sounds of Moira's cries for help. It was only a momentary relief.

The loudest noise could not drown out one's own guilty conscious.

"Wait!" Tomoiya yelled, staggering. Saliva pooled in her mouth. Attempts to swallow it back failed. She landed on her hands and knees, spitting out as much as she could between dry heaves. A burning sensation filled her throat, accompanied by the sour taste of bile. A yellow foam landed on the sand in front of her. There was a certain relief in knowing she had skipped meals earlier and wasn't spewing chunks of food. Even that was short-lived as another round of gagging left her wheezing.

Mick squatted beside her, rubbing her back. "Are you alright?"

"I didn't know," she muttered, in between involuntary spasms from dry heaves. "I didn't know she was a vampire." Tomoiya gasped for air.

"I know," Mick said. "None of us did. You don't have to go all the way down, just a little further. You can stay back with Fallin. This won't take long."

Her thoughts raced. They were close enough to see there were at least twenty men surrounding Moira.

"Are they all..."

"Purifiers," Mick said. "They are. Don't worry. She won't get away. You are completely safe."

Twenty men against one vampire wasn't safe.

Surveying the rest of the area wasn't much help. Those not involved were happy to sit on the sidelines and watch, liquor in hand. Tomoiya sighed. On a good day twenty men would be a challenge for her in vampire form. With the drug Fallin had in his bag, it was an impossibility. If they so much as suspected her, she'd be lying beside Moira, suffering the same fate.

Who left their best friend to be tortured?

She needed a plan. There had to be a way to stop the insanity. If she had a chance to talk with Fallin alone, maybe she could sway him. He had to still feel something for her.

Mick held up his hand. "That's close enough," he ordered. "Stay here with Fallin."

Tomoiya tried to focus on anything but the scene in front of them. They were too close. Vampires had strong vision, even when not in full form. Normally, improved eyesight was a welcomed trait. Tonight, however, it felt more like a curse.

It was easier to avoid what was wrong than to stand up for what was right.

Likewise, most vampires had some degree of healing ability, albeit some more than others. Moira, however, wouldn't escape tonight without physical and mental scars, if she escaped at all. Even at a distance away

48

from the scene, Tomoiya could make out the gruesome details that would haunt her for the rest of her life.

Moira was naked, bruised and bleeding. Pain radiated from her eyes as she searched for anyone to help her. Rather than aid, the trapped vampire received back glares of disgust and rounds of laughter. At that moment the girls' eyes connected. Only a few hours ago they had been best friends. What were they now?

A switch clicked. Tomoiya heard it and saw it. She witnessed the exact moment Moira accepted her fate.

If one couldn't rely on one's best friend, who else was there?

Tomoiya's stomach churned again. She forced a mouthful of acidic liquid back down, wincing at the burning sensation in her throat. Mick appeared beside Moira, blocking the view. This was her chance. Act now or accept not even trying to save a friend.

"Aren't you sad?" Tomoiya asked.

"That's not Moira anymore," Fallin replied. "That beast stole Moira from me."

"How do you know that?" Tomoiya questioned, side-eyeing Fallin. "What if Moira was a vampire for all these years? What if the Moira you love is the vampire Moira?"

"What are you talking about?!" Fallin yelled. "Do you know something? I suggest you come clean. If you are hiding..."

"No," Tomoiya interrupted. "Moira said she had something to tell me tomorrow, after she talked to you. She insisted you needed to hear it from her first. It was some sort of a secret. I just wondered if that is what she was going to tell me. That's how it happened, right? She told you she was a vampire. I mean, she didn't attack you or anything."

49

"She told me," Fallin admitted, wiping sweat from his brow with the back of his hand. "But it doesn't make a difference. Vampires are bloodthirsty beasts. It's us or them."

"Are you sure?" Tomoiya asked. "If she was always a vampire, why didn't she attack anyone?"

"Listen to me!" Fallin yelled. "You don't want others hearing you say such things."

"Ow!" Tomoiya cried. Her neck bounced back and forth. Whiplash wasn't something she wanted nor expected to experience in her lifetime. The shaking didn't stop until Fallin was done explaining the dangers associated with being labeled a supporter.

"I'm not going to tell Mick about this," Fallin said, "only because I know what you are feeling right now. We won't discuss it again."

"Okay," Tomoiya agreed, inhaling deeply. This was her final push. "But if the Moira we know is in there somewhere, don't we owe it to her to not let her suffer?"

Fallin rubbed beneath his nose as if he had a cold. He took in a deep breath of air and turned his attention back to the events unfolding further down the beach. He alternated his gaze between the sky and Moira for several minutes.

Mick had just begun his walk back when Fallin dropped the bag he was holding - lunging forward. Every gaze on the beach followed the giant as he pushed anything and anyone in his path out of his way.

Tomoiya glanced at the sack laying open. With no one watching, she crouched down and grabbed a sealed syringe. Her pocket was just big enough to stash it away.

50

A loud bang startled her into a familiar place - on her bottom. That area was becoming a bit tender. She covered her ears, clenching her eyes tightly closed. A few minutes later, a tap on her shoulder signaled it was safe to peek. Only one of her eyes was up to the challenge.

"It's okay," Mick said, glancing over his shoulder at Fallin.

Tomoiya scooted backwards. The sight of a gun in Fallin's shaking hand was enough to paint the story of the last few minutes. She wasn't sure if it was horror or fear that Mick saw in her expression. Whichever it was, it was enough to make him grab the weapon from his friend. It disappeared from her view - securely stashed in the bag beside them.

"I shouldn't be here," Tomoiya whispered. "I'm frightened. I want to go home."

"That's actually a good idea," Mick agreed. "Fallin will escort you. I have to stay and... clean things up." He motioned to Moira's body.

It was the first time she noticed her friend's body - void of all signs of life. At that moment the story became far too real. Moira was a vampire and she was dead. The party was over. Only a few stragglers remained, rushing about to wipe any evidence of their presence from the scene. What had been a loud happy party was now a death bed - a funeral empty of mourners.

"Mick," Lizelle said. "If you need anything, I'm here."

"Tomoiya is right there," Lizelle's friend whispered, loud enough to be heard. There was an undeniable amusement hidden in her words.

"So," Lizelle declared, walking away. "It's not like we're close or anything. You did know Tomoiya was best friends with that vampire, didn't you? I wouldn't be caught dead with a vampire or a monster supporter as a friend." She covered her mouth while still allowing a giggle to escape. "Caught dead might not be the best choice of words."

"Great," Mick mumbled, ignoring his groupies. "You need to go now. I have some things to tend to. I'll come see you in a couple days." A nod to Fallin relayed the rest of his message.

A shuttle ride with a murderer wasn't what she wanted to experience at the end of a difficult night, but choices were limited. In the end, getting home was what mattered the most.

Home - the only place a girl was truly safe.

Chapter Nine

The first part of the journey passed in silence. Under the circumstances, Tomoiya had no intention of trying to spark up a conversation. Talking about Moira's death could have thrown her into tears and Fallin into a rage. She'd already witnessed what he was capable of tonight. A reenactment wasn't necessary.

Mechanical noises from the shuttle's operating systems were enough to distract her. They were enough to distract anyone. Breaking down wasn't an option she had considered. The last thing she could handle was being stuck adrift with a murderer. Not just a murderer, but the man who executed her best friend.

Was a mercy killing still murder?

"I had to do it," Fallin blurted out. "There was no other way to save her. They were going to torture her until it bored them. After that, she would have been disposed of in the most painful manner."

Silence said more than words.

"A part of me wanted to believe you," Fallin admitted. "But it didn't matter. Once Mick knew she was a vampire, her fate was sealed. You don't understand how persuasive he is. It's like I'm enthralled by his words. I'm not the only one either."

"I'm surprised you did anything at all," Tomoiya barked.

"What I did, I did for you," Fallin muttered.

"For me?" Tomoiya shrieked "I didn't want you to kill her. I wanted you to save her." She bit her bottom lip drawing blood again - the pain counteracting her urge to cry. She couldn't let him find out her secret. "You know she didn't do anything evil. Why didn't you say something in her defence?"

"If Mick found out about our conversation," Fallin started. "If you had gotten involved..."

"Should I be afraid of him?" Tomoiya asked.

"Yes," Fallin answered. "I will be punished for my actions tonight in some way - better me than you."

"Punished?" Tomoiya asked. "Punished how?"

"It doesn't matter," Fallin answered. "I can take whatever he dishes out when I meet him later. I have no plans to let him know about our conversations. Perhaps I deserve whatever is to be my fate for my role in Moira's death. I don't have any answers. I am still loyal to the purifier cause."

The shuttle jerked. "Someone should fix that," Tomoiya commented. A smooth connect at a space port was something she took for granted. She stood at the metal door waiting for it to open. A hand grabbed her shoulder. Its coldness penetrated deep into her bones. Death's grip had a hold of her. Goosebumps stood at attention on her skin, saluting their creator.

"Mick always gets what he wants," Fallin said, an emptiness reflected in his eyes. It was as if his essence died with Moira on the beach, leaving only an empty shell to go through the motions of life.

Whose soul was in danger, the vampire or the man?

"He is obsessed with you," Fallin continued. "He won't ever stop until you are his. He'll stalk you to the ends of the Universe if need be. If he finds out you have any connection to vampires, he will hurt you. He may not kill you, but he will make sure you suffer."

A shiver ran down her spine. Something in his voice frightened her - something she couldn't quite put her finger on. The door opened. A quick glance back at Fallin before it closed again was all she needed to solve the puzzle.

The truth was what she had heard. The truth was what scared her.

Chapter Ten

The palace lay silent. It wasn't unusual at night for her father to still be out and the royal staff to be asleep. She sighed at the darkness. Even though she didn't need lights to see clearly, there was something comforting about walking into a lit home. A whimper from behind a door caught her attention.

The front sitting room had always been one of her favourites. It was where her father spent the most time with her. It was also where the family pet made his home.

"Hey, Little Fella," Tomoiya said, putting her hand down for him to climb up. Little Fella wasn't actually a name she would have chosen, but then he wasn't an ordinary family pet. He was a triccus.

She ran her fingers through his thick orange fur. A smile crossed her face from the memory of the day they first met...

*****

Memories...

"What is that?" Tomoiya asked. She would have pointed; however, that would break one of the rules. She wasn't sure which number, but then it wasn't the order they came in that was important.

"Stay back," her father answered. "That is a triccus. They don't particularly like any species other than their own."

"But he looks hurt!" Tomoiya cried. "I want to help him."

"Absolutely not!" her father scolded. "That one is hurt beyond your help. There are thousands of them all over. One won't be missed."

Tomoiya stared at the tiny bundle of orange fur. One eye and a nose were all that were visible There was something in that one eye that was enough to melt her heart. "I have to try!"

"Even if you did try, I doubt he would accept your help. I told you, they don't like us."

Tomoiya kicked the ground with her shoe. Her bottom lip protruded forward forming a most pathetic pout, which she matched with widened eyes. "So," she said, "you want me to break rule twenty-three?" That number she always remembered.

Rule twenty-three - a princess always tried to make a positive difference in the world around her, no matter how small.

The king sighed. "Alright," he conceded "You can try, but remember these creatures are not tame and they are not pets."

Tomoiya nodded. Her pout transformed into a smile, exposing each and every tooth possible. "Thank you," she said, heading back to grab some food for the injured triccus.

58

She stopped to catch her breath. The round trip was made in a record time by her own standards. In vampire form she wouldn't have felt a thing, but she wasn't allowed to show that side of her outside the palace walls. Tomoiya squatted in front of the tiny animal.

"Here you go, little fella," she said. "You need to eat to get better."

The triccus made a few whimpering noises as it crouched back as far away from her as possible without actually moving.

"Don't you like it?" she asked.

Another whimper.

"Are you afraid?" she asked. "I feel afraid sometimes too. Where's your mother?"

This time the creature let out a deeper cry.

"Your mother's gone, isn't she?" Tomoiya asked. "Mine is too. I bet you miss her as much as I miss mine. Maybe we could be there for each other."

The creature let out another pathetic sounding cry.

The next few days the pattern continued in a similar fashion. No matter how much food was brought, the triccus didn't touch it. One look at the condition of his fur was evidence enough his health was failing.

"You have to eat, little fella," Tomoiya said, pushing a pile of fresh food closer. "I don't know what else to do to help you."

The next visit, fear accompanied her on one side and worry on the other. Tomoiya wasn't sure what she would find when she arrived. If the little fella didn't eat something soon, he wouldn't last much longer.

She held her breath. The tiny creature lay motionless - his fur flat. He looked more like a tiny blanket than a ball. One hand covered her mouth - the other reached forward to stroke the triccus' back.

Whimpering.

"Your alive, little fella!" Tomoiya exclaimed. She glanced around. "The food, you ate it! Are you feeling better?"

Whimpering.

"Is that how you talk?" she asked. "Is that why everyone thinks you don't like them? I bet it is. Here you go, little fella. Now that you are eating again, you are probably realizing how hungry you actually are."

Whimpering.

The food disappeared from the palm of her hand quickly. The triccus brushed the side of its face against her fingers. She rewarded him with a few wiggles.

"How did you get stuck here?" she asked. "Father says triccus can't move quickly or travel long distances..."

The sight of tiny legs stopped her thoughts completely. It wasn't just the legs, but rather the shape of the triccus' feet. They looked like ten tiny pairs of ballet slippers doing point. If she hadn't known better, she might have thought there were ten ballerinas, arms linked, dancing under the coat of orange fur.

"That actually makes sense," she said, remembering the ballet lesson in which she was introduced to point. That had been the last ballet lesson she ever took. Even with her healing abilities, her toes bled for days and she swore they were traumatized for much longer. "It must hurt to go too far."

Whimpering.

"You rest, little fella," she said. "I'll be back tomorrow with some more food."

As it turned out, that trip hadn't been necessary. The next morning Tomoiya and her father found the little fella collapsed on the palace doorstep.

"Did you walk all that way?" Tomoiya asked, squatting beside the triccus. "Why did you do that?"

Whimpering.

"Can he come inside, Father?" she asked.

The king rubbed his chin. "Do you have any idea how incredible you are? You never cease to amaze me."

"Is that a yes?" Tomoiya questioned, a smile already forming.

"He can stay in the downstairs sitting room," her father stated with authority. "I don't want to see him in the sleeping quarters. If I do, he will have to go."

Tomoiya leaped forward, embracing her father around the waist. "Thank you," she said, beaming with joy.

*****

She felt soft fur nudging her fingers. "Sorry, Little Fella," she said. "I was lost in memories. At least they were happy ones. It's been a bad day."

Whimpering.

"I knew you'd understand," she muttered. "I'm a little tired. Maybe we should go to bed."

Over the years they had learned to understand little bits of each other's language. Bed was one word her triccus knew well. He scurried off to a pillow bed in one corner and made himself comfortable. He made a few noises Tomoiya identified as *sleep well.*

Language - the basis for understanding. If communication was possible, common ground was easier to find.

"Good night," she whispered, heading to her room.

Her bed was a welcome sight. She flopped down without changing. Her hands fumbled for her favourite bear. Looking into its blank stare, she mumbled, "I'm going to need your help tonight."

Tears.

Chapter Eleven

Pain.

Tomoiya screamed. Her scalp felt like it was on fire. She tried to reach back to release her hair from whatever it was caught on, but her arms wouldn't move. She tried again - nothing.

"Help!" she cried.

"Shut up, vampire scum."

It was a familiar voice, but she couldn't put a face to it. "Where am I? Who are you?" She felt a sharp pain on one side.

"You were told to shut up."

The second voice she recognized. A glob of spit hit her face. She shook her head, trying to get rid of the slimy feeling. "Fallin? What's going on?"

"Did you think you could hide being a vampire from us forever?" he asked. "All vampires are going to get what's coming to them. You are going to be the perfect example to show the Universe."

Pain.

"Please stop," she begged. "You're hurting me!"

Laughter.

"You don't know the meaning of hurting yet."

"Mick?" She didn't need to ask. She knew it was him. Her eyes began to focus, surveying the surroundings. There was a large bonfire to one side of her. She could hear water moving in the distance.

She spat out a mouthful of sand that had been kicked in her face. Her eyes stung. There was nothing she could do. Other than rolling her head from side to side, she couldn't move.

Another kick landed hard. Her clothes tore. Screams were met with ridicule. Faces became clearer. They were Mick's friends. She was back on the beach where Moira had died.

"No!" she yelled, using every ounce of her energy to try to move. Nothing happened. Another mouthful of sand found its way inside her mouth. She couldn't spit it out fast enough.

Gasping for air, she searched the faces for anyone who would help. Her closest friends stood and watched, not picking up a finger to try to help - their expressions emotionless. There had to be someone who would help her. Her gaze passed Mick's face, then Fallin's, before coming to rest on one she knew better than any.

"Moira," she muttered, still spitting out sand. "Help me. Don't let them hurt me like this."

Indescribable pain was her only reward. Moira looked away, as if that made it all right not to take action.

She screamed!

"Tomoiya!" her father yelled. "It's just a dream." He pulled her head to his chest and embraced her.

"A dream," Tomoiya echoed, still gasping for air. But it wasn't just a dream. That was how Moira must have felt. She was as guilty as anyone else for letting her best friend die. Now she knew what it was like to be on the opposite side. Everything Moira experienced was more painful knowing her closest friends - the people she trusted and loved, abandoned her.

Her heart raced, not showing any signs of slowing down. Sweat trickled down, adding more moisture to her already soaked clothes.

"Child," her father whispered. "What has frightened you this much?"

"I didn't know," she mumbled. "She never told me."

"What didn't you know?"

"Moira," she said. "I didn't know she was a vampire. She never told me. I had no clue all this time."

"She told you?" the king asked.

"She's dead," Tomoiya cried. "They killed her."

"Who killed her?"

"Purifiers," Tomoiya answered. She shook her head. "It was Mick and Fallin."

He pulled her close again. "Relax," he said. "Don't think about anything. I'm here with you."

Eventually, the shaking stopped and her breathing returned to normal. Goosebumps lined her arms - not out of fear, but rather a sign of the chill she felt from wet clothing.

"You should wash up and change," her father suggested. "Then meet me in my study. I need to know everything that happened tonight."

That was the first time she had heard fear in her father's voice. He tried to hide it, but it was there nonetheless.

More secrets.

Chapter Twelve

The study was her father's place to think. Whenever a problem or issue arose, you'd find the king behind his desk, usually rubbing his temples. On the wall above his chair, Tomoiya's almost life-size portrait hung. She had been sixteen at the time - a world away from where she stood today.

Everyone adored the large white hoop-style dress she wore, including a young boy's small piglet that had escaped and hid beneath layers of skirt. The smile portrayed in the painting was a direct result of watching the finest of her personal guard chasing the pig around, unable to catch it.

In the end, the general of the royal fleets caught up to it. He was rewarded with a spraying of urine that ruined his best uniform. The pig was returned to the boy, who agreed never to bring a pet to a royal celebration again. For the rest of the evening, Tomoiya was barely able to contain herself. Although she managed not to snicker too much, she couldn't contain the grin that spanned her entire face.

"Have a seat," the king requested.

Tomoiya complied, biting her lip. He may have been her father, but in the study, he was the King. Even a princess was merely one of his subjects. She couldn't even fathom the day she would sit behind that desk as queen. As an only child it was her destiny - one she hoped was a very long way away.

"Where do you want me to start?" Tomoiya asked, the syringe she stole from the Purifiers locked between her fingers.

Her father sighed. "I've seen a good deal of it," he answered.

"How?"

Her father pressed a button and a clear rectangle appeared between them. She frowned at the picture that formed.

"Citizens of the civilized worlds," Mick said. "We come to you in the wake of a tragedy. A personal friend of mine has been taken away from us in a brutal attack."

"But..."

The king held up one hand, silencing her.

"During a graduation celebration, a vampire surfaced. Moira, of the Transilva Galaxy, transformed in public and attacked an ordinary citizen."

A video close-up of Moira's face appeared. Her head thrashed back and forth, saliva flowing freely out of her open mouth. The noises she made sounded more beast than those of an intelligent species.

"As you can see," Mick continued, "she was completely mad. The vampire gene had taken over completely. Her eyes transformed and fangs were fully extended. We could barely contain her. Luckily, my family has been developing a drug for generations. By separating the monster gene, we were able to paralyze the subject. It was our hope to turn her over to the New World Alliance. Unfortunately, that wasn't possible. Fallin, of Mancray, the one who first encountered the beast, unbeknownst to myself, had been bitten. It is believed that when he began to change, he lost the ability for reasonable thought."

The video footage focused on Fallin rushing down the beach, knocking over anything in his path. The gun fired.

"He then threw her body in the bonfire, before fleeing," Mick explained. "It was unfortunate I only kept one dose of the drug in my possession. I'd like to take credit for his demise. It was, however, not of our doing. I found his body aboard a shuttle orbiting Moira's homeworld. An object had pierced his heart and he had been decapitated. Not a drop of blood was present. We can only assume Moira's family was somehow involved. I have been given a license to test them for the vampire gene. Preparations are already underway."

Tomoiya gasped. Her head fell between her knees. She barely heard the click of the screen turning off over her own heartbeat.

"The rest sounds like an ad for an exterminator," the king said.

"That's not what happened," Tomoiya said. "Fallin dropped me off. He was going to meet Mick."

"You used the word purifier," her father said.

"Yes," Tomoiya answered. "That's what Mick said they were. There were over twenty of them." She placed the syringe on the desk. "And they had a lot more of the drug too."

"How did you get this?!" the king demanded.

"I stole it," Tomoiya admitted. "When no one was looking. I had to do something. It was just sitting there."

"Do you know how dangerous that was?!" her father yelled. "Those boys could have killed you."

"I know," Tomoiya said. "Whatever that is, it forces our real selves to surface as well as paralyzing from the neck down."

"Are you sure?"

"I wish I wasn't," Tomoiya muttered. "I wish today had never happened."

"Today is over," her father said.

"No," Tomoiya replied. "At least not for me. I watched Moira being tortured and beaten. She begged for my help and I did nothing. What kind of a person does that make me?"

"An alive one," her father offered. "You couldn't have fought them all, especially with the threat of that drug. It should ease your mind that her death wasn't in vain. This sample could save thousands of lives."

"I thought you were mad at me for taking it."

"I am," the king said. "But I am proud of you as well. Let's not take any more chances though, okay?"

Tomoiya nodded.

"Now, perhaps we can discuss where you got that ring," her father said, pointing to her finger with the syringe.

"I almost forgot with everything that was happening," Tomoiya answered. "Mick gave it to me."

"And you agreed to wear it?"

"Not exactly," Tomoiya answered slowly, giving her enough time to carefully choose her next words. "He announced to the whole graduating class I had agreed to marry him without actually asking me. I thought it was better not to cause a scene. I was going to give it back to him when we were alone, but then Moira..."

The king rubbed his chin. His jaw cracked, making a loud popping noise. "I was going to send you to your new school in a few weeks," he said. He closed his eyes, pausing for a moment. "Under the circumstances, that won't be possible. Go pack. You will be leaving immediately." Before she had a chance to speak, he added, "There is no room for discussion."

Another wall forced the mouse to turn, but what was waiting around the corner?

Chapter Thirteen

"General," the king said, "please have a seat."

"Is this a formal meeting or personal?" the general asked, still standing at attention.

"A little of both," the king admitted. "Jeigns, I find myself in a familiar situation once again. I need your help."

The general nodded. His lips pressed firmly together, forming a seal that wasn't ready to be broken. The invitation to sit, however, was accepted.

"I assume you've watched the video," the king continued. "We have a problem." He tossed the ring onto his desk.

Jeigns took a seat. "This boy has been a problem before. I am sure you can handle it."

"Not this time," the king replied. "He is claiming to be a direct descendant of one of the Purifiers."

"Are you sure?"

"Quite," the king answered. His body leaned over part of the desk. "I don't need to tell you - history repeats itself. If this boy has Woden's blood, he will not rest until she is his. Without even knowing why, he'll stalk her to the ends of the Universe."

"Does she know?" Jeigns asked.

"No," the king said. "I had hoped to have time to explain everything before sending her off to school. Unfortunately, that won't be the case."

"So you've decided to send her into the dark?" Jeigns raised an eyebrow. "You do know things have changed since you were last an active member of society in that area, don't you? There are rumours of uprisings from within the vampire empire itself."

"Within?"

"Yes," the general said. "I've had my ears open since you first began considering sending Tomoiya there. There are new levels of vampires, their rank based on blood percentages."

"What do you mean? Explain yourself!" the king demanded.

"The race of vampires at one point in history kept to itself. No one could have anticipated problems arising from mating with other species. Woden, during the war, created a mass migration. Our kind took up homes spanning thousands of worlds."

"I already knew all this," the king said. "There was no problem when Tomoiya's mother and I left."

"No," the general admitted. "May I, Duran?" He pointed to a small wooden box containing the finest cigars in existence.

74

"Of course," the king answered. He reached inside his bottom drawer and pulled out a flask of purple liquid and two glasses. He filled each one halfway before offering his general and closest friend one.

"Thank you," Jeigns said, the glass raised in the air. One swig emptied the contents. "It's true the first few generations no one noticed anything. It seems the problem only becomes apparent if the percentage of vampire blood in an offspring slips under fifty percent."

"I'm not sure I understand," the king admitted.

"The vampire gene is dominant and it remains dominant no matter how small a fragment is present in an individual," the general answered. "The effect of the vampire gene stretching to remain the most influential causes a previously unforeseen type of mutation. The symptoms deteriorate each time the gene is, for lack of a better way to say it, split."

"Deteriorate how?" the king asked, offering a flame to light the general's cigar.

"As I said, it isn't noticeable until an individual is under fifty percent vampire. Then it begins. A decline in reasoning abilities and intelligence, as well as a more primal behaviour are two key traits. There is also a change in appearance while in vampire form."

"How does this affect us?" Duran asked.

"There is a division in the ranks. Pure bloods and rank one or two vampires have more power," the general answered. "The lower ranks want that power or at least some form of equality. We are a species corrupt from within."

"And how many levels are there?" the king asked.

"At last I heard, a level twelve had been discovered."

"A level twelve?" the king bellowed. "Good orbits, what would that even be like?"

"A beast," the general replied, blowing a ring of smoke. "They are said to have no intellect at all, relying entirely on instincts. They look and act like animals, surviving off of blood and flesh of prey. And appearance... well, let's just say greyish colour skin and eyes pitch black aren't very appealing. The only ones they respond to in any way at all are those from their own bloodlines."

"If I am hearing correctly, Woden brought into existence a false image of vampires in order to start a war. By doing so he, in fact, created the very beast he fabricated in the first place." the king said.

"Ironic, isn't it?" the general asked. "There hasn't been a report of an uprising yet, but that doesn't mean Tomoiya is completely safe. You know, once inside the college, I will not be able to intervene."

"Yes," the king answered, swirling the green liquid in his glass before emptying it into his mouth. "But I fear anything is safer than here. As you know, the college moves around as part of its security protocol. Only the elders know its exact location."

"And what of the other species?" the general asked.

The king sighed. "I have always hoped that the different races of the Universe would find a way to co-exist. It seems that is more fantasy than reality. There is little I can do about that. Her identity and race will be hidden - as will everyone else's there. She should be fine until I can sort things out."

"How much will she know before we leave?" Jeigns asked.

"As much as I have time to tell her," the king answered. "She is packing at the moment."

76

"Why so quickly?"

Duran sighed. "Technology, I hate it. It is, however, an indispensable evil we all must live with. Nowadays just about everything can be traced. Just last week I read about a new system with the ability to track space displacement created by moving objects."

"You are worried he will follow her," the general said.

"If he can," the king replied, "I have no doubt he will. I want as little traces of where she went left as possible. There can be nothing left to chance. If Mick suspects something is wrong, you can bet he will be watching for any move. Tomoiya needs to be gone before that can happen."

Knocking.

"Sire," the king's attendant said. "I have a delivery for you." He placed a letter on the king's desk, bowed and exited.

"Is that..."

"From Mick," the king blurted out. It was several minutes before he ripped open the envelope. "He's asking for a meeting to discuss a wedding. Looks like my talk with Tomoiya just became a whole lot shorter. I hate to have to leave things for you to take care of, but I'm afraid I have no choice."

"I understand," Jeigns said, nodding.

"And general," the king added. "You may not be able to help Tomoiya at college, but if Mick crosses into the other side of the Universe, you'll be her first line of defence. I'm counting on you to never let him find her."

"You know I think of her as family," the general answered. "I would die protecting her."

Duran scribbled on a blank piece of paper. "These are the coordinates for the drop-off. Enter them yourself and only after you are well into the dark."

"You don't trust our men?" the general asked.

The king sighed. "It isn't them. I'm not taking any chances. Things left to fate tend to have unexpected results."

Jeigns nodded.

The king's fingers trembled, holding a package wrapped in brown paper retrieved from the top drawer of his desk. "Please give this to her," he requested. "There won't be enough time for me to explain everything and too many questions. Tomoiya can be a stubborn girl."

"I have no idea where she got that trait from," Jeigns said, taking the package.

The king chuckled. "Indeed." The two shook hands followed by an embrace. "Keep my daughter safe. She's all I have."

"Might I suggest a tightening of security here as well?" Jeigns asked. "Keep in mind, Tomoiya feels the same way about you as you do about her."

Chapter Fourteen

Tomoiya sat on her bed, watching her aids rush about packing all the things she might need while at college. Not once did anyone ask her opinion about what to take or leave behind.

A strong independent woman who has everything decided for her.

She couldn't blame them, they were only following orders. She needed to be packed - yesterday. She flopped backwards and covered her face with a pillow. Forgetting about that ring was a big mistake - one she was paying for now.

"Tomoiya," Martina called. "Stop messing around and change. You are going to be travelling for a long time. It would be best to be comfortable."

A long way to nowhere.

"How am I supposed to decide what to wear if I don't even know where I am going?" Tomoiya complained. She stashed the teddy bear from her bed in amongst her belongings.

"Casual," Martina answered. "You can change when you arrive. Your father is waiting. The longer you dawdle, the less time you'll have with him before you leave."

Martina was right, of course. It was often the case - if she did what she was told right away, she would have more time with her father. Even if it was only a few minutes, over years, those minutes added up - not that she actually kept track.

Tomoiya pulled on an oversized shirt and comfortable pants. Normally, she wouldn't be seen in such an outfit outside her room, but if it was as far away as she imagined, proper dress would become uncomfortable, not to mention wrinkled.

Arriving at the study door with Little Fella in her arms, she barely missed bumping into the general of her royal fleet on his way out. His nonchalant bow in her direction was enough to tip her off to new orders having been issued by her father.

"He can't go with you," her father declared from inside the study.

She peeked round the corner. "You aren't even looking at me," she scoffed.

The king turned around. He alternated his glance between his daughter and the triccus. "I know you far too well," he said, shaking his head. "You can't take a pet on this journey."

"You'll look after him?" Her fingers ran through his orange fur. There are things a girl can't tell her father, or aids. In that respect, Little Fella was her last living confidant.

"Of course," her father answered. As a king he would never admit it publicly, but that triccus had become just as much a part of the family to him as it had to his daughter.

"Are you going to tell me where I am going?" Tomoiya blurted out. "Everyone is acting as if it is very far."

"Sit," the king ordered. "There are some things I perhaps should have told you before. Unfortunately, there isn't time to go over everything. What you need to know is that there is another side to the Universe - one from where our race originated. Your mother and I were both born there."

Tomoiya gasped. Her mouth opened, but she was silenced by her father before a single noise had a chance to manifest. As much as she wanted to yell at him for hiding something so important, she also needed to hear him out.

Lies - a necessary evil or a requirement for safety?

"We refer to it as the dark side simply because it is darker there. The suns in every solar system are tinted reds, blues and purples mainly. The further in you travel, the darker the colour. Our kingdom actually extends well into it. Keeping our borders closed has helped me to keep that bit of information... in the dark." He chuckled, turning his laugh into a cough after realizing he was the only one amused.

"Why?"

"Your mother and I disagreed with some of the politics going on at the time. We didn't want to abandon our principals. Of course, we left on good terms. The Gathering of the Elders always wanted us to return. That's why it has been easy for me to arrange your education. It's a royal-level institution with more than adequate security."

Locked to keep others out or students in?

"Your identity will remain hidden, along with your race," the king continued. "Those rules prevent any prejudices from surfacing. Everyone is equal."

Until identities surfaced... the names might have changed but the game was the same.

"Why this particular school?" Tomoiya muttered.

"It's where your mother and I met," the king admitted. "It has some emotional value to me. I thought it might to you as well. You may learn a bit about her during your stay and perhaps a bit about yourself as well."

A child deserved to know her mother. School wasn't the place to learn such things - home was.

"When can I come back?" Tomoiya asked.

"I'm not sure," the king mumbled. "We have a palace located on the far reaches of our kingdom. It will be made ready for you. There will be no way for us to communicate until you reach there. Messages are too easy to trace."

Knocking.

"Sire," the king's attendant said. "A courier has been sent for a response. He appears to be quite anxious."

"Tell him I'll be a few minutes," the king ordered.

"Very good, Sire."

"I have to go now, don't I?" Tomoiya asked.

"Yes," her father answered, embracing her. "I wish it wasn't so soon. I'll have things cleared up as fast as I can."

"What if you can't?"

"I don't know," he answered. "Let me worry about it for now." His lips brushed her forehead.

A royal goodbye. Rule number one - a princess never cried in public.

"General Paradi," the king said, breaking the embrace. "Please come in. Tomoiya was just leaving for school."

Paradi bowed with precision, his hand covering his heart. "Your highnesses," he said, keeping his head bowed.

"Rise," the king ordered.

If one looked up the meaning of the word perfectionist, a picture of the general of the king's royal fleet was bound to be there. When it came to his job, everything was by-the-book and his job was everything to him.

Jeigns, on the other hand, had personality. There was a certain amount of relief that accompanied the realization that he was the one escorting her to her new existence.

It was the little things that made life worth living.

Tomoiya's back pushed against the wall outside her father's study. Her cheeks puffed out - her lips allowing only minute amounts of air to pass through them in a steady stream. This was really happening. One night was all it took to lose everything.

Death - a finality. Perhaps there was a connection between loss of life and loss of all reasons for living. Was simply being alive enough? Rule forty-two - a princess never gave up on life.

"I want all borders secured. Tighten everything up," the king ordered. "Send out messages to our people living outside the thirteen galaxies. They are to return if they want our protection. Make it within forty-eight hours. After that they are on their own."

"Yes Sire," the general answered.

"The old palace," the king started. "I want it functional again. You'll escort the princess' personal aids to prepare it for her needs."

There was no doubt about the finality in his voice. She glanced around the hall, knowing this was the last time she would see her home again.

Chapter Fifteen

"Tomoiya," Jeigns called. "It's time to wake up."

"Where are we?" she asked.

"As far as I am allowed to take you," Jeigns answered. "You have to transfer to a special shuttle. Students travel together to the final destination. Your belongings have already been sent ahead."

"Any advice?" Tomoiya mumbled amidst a yawn.

"Yes," the general answered, "cover your mouth when it is that wide open. I believe one of the rules applies to that."

Rule ninety-six - a princess always displayed immaculate manners.

Tomoiya threw off her blanket. Glancing down at her outfit, she chuckled. "I didn't have a chance to change. With these clothes, I doubt anyone will notice me yawning. I'm pretty sure I'm breaking at least ten rules simply by being seen."

The general side-eyed her. "While it is against my vows to speak ill of my princess, I can't deny your statement."

She barely caught an apple tossed through the air in her direction. "Hey," she complained.

"You flinched," Jeigns said, turning away. "A lady doesn't flinch nor does she say *hey*. Perhaps, I have been too lenient with your training."

Tomoiya raised her upper lip and mimicked repeating the general's words - following it up with an overzealous eye-roll.

"I saw that," he said. "You aren't a child anymore."

"I don't think I ever was," she replied.

"You are royalty and with that title comes responsibility."

Responsibility to who? To herself; her father; Moira...

"This is serious, Tomoiya," the general barked. "For the first time, you are going to truly be on your own. No one will be there to remind you of these things. You never have a second chance to make a first impression."

"Well then," she said, "I'm already in trouble." She pointed to her clothing. She sighed. "Don't worry. I'll be fine."

She shifted her weight back and forth, alternating between legs. A full neck rotation became added to the mix.

"There is a rule about fidgeting," the general said, standing perfectly still at the closed door.

"There is a rule for everything," Tomoiya answered. "Besides, I wasn't fidgeting. I was limbering. Didn't you tell me that was necessary?"

"Before exercising, yes," the general said. "I'm not sure walking across a space bridge between ships counts as exercise."

The door opened before she had a chance to continue the argument. She peeked in before stepping through across the threshold. Going on a spacewalk wasn't one of her favourite activities. In her opinion, anything could go wrong. It was, after all, nothing more than a pressurized tube locked between doors. The slightest miscalculation and she would end up floating away - a tiny spec of space debris.

It didn't matter how fast she tried to move, every step on the white material felt like an eternity. She lurched forward, taking the last few steps all at once. Tripping over her own feet, she grabbed the door frame with a bear hug. Her arms fell to her sides convinced her legs had fully recovered.

Looking back, she watched the door to her ship close, Jeigns still standing in the same spot watching. His part in this trip was successfully completed. She was on her own now.

On her own was exactly what she was. The shuttle was made up of rows and rows of seats - all empty. The first section seemed a good enough choice - although technically she had her pick of seats since there was no one present to greet her or assign her a spot.

She flopped back in a chair, making herself comfortable. There was no indication of how long she had to sit and wait, or even what came next. None of that mattered though.

Looking down at the Journal clenched in her grip, Tomoiya smiled. She opened it to the first page. Her fingers caressed the pure white paper. A sign, maybe even from her mother. Wherever it came from, she'd been given a clean slate. A place where her story could begin. This time she'd make sure it had a happy ending.

Author's Message

I hope you have enjoyed reading *Collecting Tears* as much as I have writing it. Watch for new books in this series coming soon.

ABOUT THE AUTHOR

C.A. King is the recipient of several awards, including: The Hamilton Spectator Readers' Choice Award for 2017 Best Author; The Brant News Readers' Choice Award for 2017 Best Author; Readers' Favourite award in the short story/novella category; the 2017 SIBA Award for Best New Adult; and the 2017 SIBA Award for Best Novella.

Currently residing in Brantford, Ontario Canada, she lives with her two sons. She began her writing career after the tragic loss of her parents and husband. Redirecting her emotions through writing became therapeutic in her battle with depression and in 2014 she decided to publish some of her works.

Other Titles from C.A. King

The Portal Prophecies

These great titles in C.A. King's The Portal Prophecies series are available now at most online book retailers:

A Keeper's Destiny

A Halloween's Curse

Frost Bitten

Sleeping Sands

Deadly Perceptions

Finding Balance

Volume I Books 1-3

Volume II Books 4-6

The prophecies are the key to their survival. Can they solve them in time?

Shattering the Effects of Time

Join the Shinning brothers, Jessie, Dezi and Pete as they set out on a quest to save their younger sister. No magic known to them or their friends has ever been able to reverse the grip of time. A few legends, however, exist mentioning ancient items that may hold the key to do exactly that.

This brand new series will take you on a search for the Fountain of Youth and Mermaids; a quest for the Holy Grail; a trip to visit Daryl the mountain guru, in the hunt for the Cinamani Stone; on a search for Ambrosia, the food of the Gods; and other adventures.

Surviving the Sins: Answering the Call

The prophecies are being rewritten. This time someone is using the seven deadly sins: Lust; Gluttony; Greed; Sloth; Wrath; Envy; and Pride, to unlock an ancient evil. The book falls into Jade's hands to answer destiny's call. Can she survive the sins?

Surviving the Sins: Pride

No one is safe when a witch's pride is at stake.

Prudance is back in Pewterclaw, and she isn't about to give up her prestigious status without a fight - especially not because of vampires. As an eighth-generation witch, she plans to do whatever it takes to stop the proposed new legislation from becoming law, including waking the dead for help.

Humility isn't in her vocabulary. With an ego spinning out of control and ancestral power at her fingertips, Prudance weaves a plot to keep Jade and Gavin separated. Will it be enough to satisfy the spirits she summoned?

When her pride costs more than she bargained for, someone has to pay the tab - but who will it be?

Surviving the Sins: Lust

What Mother doesn't know won't hurt her.

Lucinda has spent her entire existence running The Organization and looking after Mother's needs without complaint. That's about to change. A burning desire had manifested inside her - one she could no longer deny... Lust.

When Constable Safron Black shows up unexpected with news of an imprisoned God, Lucinda unravels. With power fuelling her passion, she'll do anything to make Morynx her mate.

****

Jade and her friends find themselves at a standstill. They have already failed to stop Pride from completing its task and they haven't located any victims for the other six sins. A strange fire in the municipal office puts them hot on the trail of what could be answers. Will they be in time to stop the dial from moving and further opening the way for Morynx?

When Leaves Fall: A Different Point of View Story

Ralph wakes up to what others only experience in a nightmare. Chained to a shed, he has no idea where he is, or who his captor is. His memories a blurred at best. As the days press on he finds himself experiencing a roller coaster of feelings. Hunger, thirst and pain become his only companions. Flashbacks of a happier time are all he has to keep him going. As his situation deteriorates, he finds himself doubting the very things he wants most - a family.

When Leaves Fall is a dramatic-thriller with a twist. Keep the tissue box close for the ending.

Tomoiya's Story

A Vampire Tale. She had a secret but she wasn't the only one who had something to hide.

Book I ~ Escape to Darkness

Book II ~ Collecting Tears

Book III~ Coming Soon

Peach Coloured Daisies: A Cursed by the Gods Story

He couldn't die. An ancient curse meant she always did. This time, that was going to change - one way or another.

When Daisy's grandmother, her last living relative, passes away, she doesn't know where to turn. Things go from bad to worse when a local psychic tells her about a curse. Alone and confused, she ends up in front of her college professor's office, ready to cry her heart out in his arms.

Matt Demi might be the son of a God, but he's living the life of a cursed man. He's had to watch the woman he loves die on her twenty-first birthday countless times. Nothing he does seems to be able to affect the outcome. When she shows up at his office scared out of her wits by a psychic's prediction, he vows this time will be different.

With only three days, Matt will need to embrace a side of him he swore off long ago to save her, but will he lose himself in the process?

Flower Shields: A Four Horsemen Novel

Meet the four horsemen: Michael, Gabrielle, Uriel and Raphael. For centuries their job has been to guard the gates of hell, making sure they never open. Without the keys, there was never any real threat. That's about to change. There are rumours on the horizon that demon followers unearthed scrolls that explain exactly how to find the lost keys. This new battle is a race to see which side locates them first.

Michael couldn't care less about the love story behind how and why the world was created. In fact, nothing matters to him other than keeping the gates to hell closed. If one of the lost keys ever fell into the wrong hands, all humanity would be doomed. He's not going to let that happen - at any cost.

****

Tara's life is nothing short of a disaster. She's managed to flunk out of college with about the same amount of dignity as every relationship she's been in. The only constant in her life has been her love for flowers. When she's attacked at work, a stranger comes to her aid. Michael might be good-looking, but he's also arrogant, bossy and crazy. He's also her only chance to figure out who attacked her and why. Should she follow her heart and trust him - or listen to her head and run?

Drawing Strength From Words: A Four Horsemen Novel

Meet the four horsemen: Michael, Gabrielle, Uriel and Raphael.

For centuries their sole purpose has been guarding the sealed gates to hell. Without keys, there was never any real threat. That was about to change...

For Gabrielle, protecting mankind was merely a job for which she received little credit. The vast insecurities of men altered history itself, portraying her as a masculine brute. Taking a back seat to her brothers seemed the right thing to do, but left a bitter taste in her mouth and an impenetrable barricade shielding her heart.

****

Ryder bounced around the system from the moment both his parents were killed. Between that and run-ins with the law for crimes he never committed, it seemed the whole world was conspiring against him. Never growing attached to anyone was rule number one: a rule he'd never broken until a white-haired vixen, with blocks of ice on her shoulders, walked right into his life. Melting through those frosty layers became all that mattered, even if that meant sacrificing himself in the process.

Miracles Not Included

A heartfelt romantic story about: life; love; loss; and learning to love again. If only life came with instructions and a warning label ~ Miracles Not Included.

****

Chris was born to be a writer. Even the smallest of details couldn't pass without notice, often becoming part of a plot for her next novel. The one thing she never saw coming was her husband's sudden illness.

Jason loved his wife from the moment they met. Nothing could ever change that - nothing except the death sentence he'd been handed - a terminal cancer diagnosis.

His story was ending: Hers was starting a new chapter and more than one miracle was needed to turn the page.

Twisted Tales of a Dead End Street

A paranormal mystery laced with comedic undertones: Twisted Tales of a Dead End Street.

Nine neighbours were invited to the mysterious dinner party at 9 Nine Street. Their host, the owner of the mansion, had more planned for the evening than just roast beef. When the secret of their quiet street was revealed, everything changed, blurring the lines between the tangible and the paranormal.

Was the number nine the difference between life and death? Would any of them survive long enough to uncover the truth? They would each soon find out this wasn't a simple case of who-done-it so much as one of what was being done and by whom.

Shot Through The Heart: A Faerie Tale

A tale of two worlds - one filled with magic; the other void of it. But what happened to those trapped between the two? Adelia was about to find out...

Magic and structure were the foundations of her existence. Temptation controlled the ability to destroy everything she knew. The world of men held a powerful allure over her heart, waking that which had long been dormant. It enticed her, snagging her in a web of emotions.

A decision had to be made. Was feeling love for the first time worth sacrificing magic and immortality?